TAKAO AND GRANDFATHER'S SWORD

Takao and Grandfather's Sword

YOSHIKO UCHIDA

Illustrated by William M. Hutchinson

HOUGHTON MIFFLIN COMPANY

BOSTON

| Atlanta | Dallas | Geneva, Illinois |
| Palo Alto | Princeton | Toronto |

Houghton Mifflin Edition, 1993

Printed in the U.S.A.

ISBN 0-395-61815-0

3456789-B-96 95 94 93

*For my friends
in the Folk Art Movement of Japan*

PREFACE

When I first wrote TAKAO AND GRANDFATHER'S SWORD in 1958, I had recently returned from two years in Japan on a Ford Foundation Fellowship. I had gone in search of more folktales for my next collection, but became just as interested in the world of Japanese crafts—especially pottery.

I got to know several fine potters who lived in Kyoto and visited their workshops and kilns. I also liked exploring the many curio and antique shops of the city and sometimes even found wonderful old pottery or sword guards I could buy.

When I was ready to write my next book, the father turned out to be a potter, and of course I found a way to get Takao into an antique shop.

Japan has undergone enormous changes in the years since I first wrote this book, but I know there are still many potters in Kyoto creating beautiful pottery, and I hope there are still young boys there who treasure old samurai swords.

Y. U.
September 1991

CONTENTS

TAKAO AND GRANDFATHER'S SWORD

ONE

The Big Order

Takao slid open the front door and called out as he slipped his schoolbag from his shoulder. *"Tadaima! I'm home!"*

He kicked off his shoes and then noticed the shiny black pair placed neatly together at the entrance. He groaned softly and wrinkled his nose. Those stiff shoes, still smelling of shoe polish, could belong only to Mr. Kato—horrible Mr. Kato with his round black glasses, his pale unfriendly face, and the mustache that twitched when he was annoyed. Once each month he came with orders for Father's pottery from the three finest shops on Gojo Hill, and each time he left, Father was unhappy and cross.

"Why do you bother with that old Kato-san, anyway?" Takao had asked once.

But Father had said, "I'm afraid he is quite necessary, Takao. Although he is disagreeable, he does bring me many fine orders for my pottery."

Takao wished now that he had come in silently so he might tiptoe past the sitting room without going in. But it was too late, for Mother called out to him. "Come in, Taka-chan," she said. "Kato-san is here."

Takao saw that Mother had taken down the good silk cushions from the closet and was serving tea with her best porcelain tea set. She had even taken off the big white apron she usually wore, so Takao could see all of her *kimono* for a change. Somehow Mother didn't look like Mother without the apron she always wore, and even Father looked different. He stared glumly down at the *tatami* and ran a hand over his short-cropped hair. It was not like Father to look so sad and troubled.

Takao knelt to the floor and bowed. "Good afternoon," he murmured, but he was careful not to lower his head too far. After all, he did not want to show Mr. Kato too much respect.

Mr. Kato glanced at Takao over the rim of his glasses and nodded briefly. Then, he turned to speak to Father as though Takao was worth no more attention than a fly on the wall. Mr. Kato could not be bothered with little ten-year-old boys wearing dusty black uniforms worn thin at the knees. Takao decided then and there that he would never speak again to this haughty, rude man.

"Well, Sakata-san," Mr. Kato said brusquely to Father, "can you make the twenty-five tea sets by the first of November or not?"

Takao knew Father was troubled. He rubbed his chin and looked down into his teacup. "*Sah . . .*" he said slowly. "That is not very much time. It is difficult because I work alone, and you must remember it is necessary for me to make many more pots besides your tea sets in order to fill up the kiln. I cannot afford to fire a kiln that is not fully loaded."

"But this is a special order," Mr. Kato interrupted. "It will bring you a good price. I offer you a fine opportunity, but if you do not wish it . . ."

"Of course, I wish it," Father said. "It just seems unreasonable to ask for twenty-five tea sets in less than three weeks. Besides, if the weather is not good, the pots will not dry. There are many things to be considered."

Mr. Kato scowled and his face grew red, and Takao thought he looked like an angry dragon. He grinned as he pictured Mr. Kato with a thorny green tail and several more pair of legs.

But Mr. Kato was not smiling at all. "If you must know," he said grumbling, "this is an order for a gentleman who sails for America on November second. We must have the tea sets by the first so he can see them before he leaves."

"I see," Father murmured, but he still looked troubled.

Mother glanced at Father and then spoke to Mr. Kato herself.

"I think we can do it," she said. "At any rate, we shall do our best, Kato-san. We shall try very hard to finish the sets by November first."

She filled Mr. Kato's cup and smiled cheerfully. "And now, Kato-san," she urged, "please, won't you have more tea?"

Not many people could stay angry when Mother, with her pretty round face, offered such a friendly smile. Mr. Kato seemed satisfied with her words and nodded briefly.

"Very well," he said. "I shall tell the owner of

our shops that you can meet his demands. He will be pleased."

"It is a difficult demand," Father said quietly. "He must be a difficult man."

If Mr. Kato heard Father, he pretended he had not. He rose and stepped over to inspect the *samurai* sword displayed in the special alcove of the room. He bent for a closer look and then picked it up to examine it more carefully.

"That's mine!" Takao said quickly, forgetting that he had decided not to speak another word to Mr. Kato. "Grandfather left it for me."

"We call it Takao's treasure," Mother said, smiling. "He is very proud of it."

"And he should be," Mr. Kato agreed. "It is a fine sword."

Once more, he ignored Takao and spoke to Father. "If you should ever wish to sell this sword," he said, "I would pay a good price for it." He ran his hand along the carved scabbard of the sword as though he would like very much to own it.

"Takao's grandfather left it to him when he died three years ago," Father explained. "I do not believe he wishes to sell it."

"I don't!" Takao said clearly. "It's not for sale at all. I'm never going to sell it!"

Mr. Kato bared his gold teeth and laughed in Takao's direction. "Ha, the small one speaks with a loud tongue," he said in a mocking tone. "But some-day, he may change his mind, and when he does, you will let me know."

I'd never, never sell it to you, Takao thought grimly, and when Mr. Kato was safely out of the house, he turned to Father and said, "I'll never let that old dragon have my beautiful sword!"

Father nodded. "You are quite right, my son," he said. And he went out to his workshop without even telling Takao that Mr. Kato should not be called names behind his back.

Takao followed him out to the workshop. "Is it a very big order, Father?" he asked.

"It is a very big order," Father answered. "And I do not like to work in such haste. It is not wise to hurry the making of a beautiful thing."

Takao watched Father sit at the potter's wheel and place a ball of gray clay in the center. Now, with his foot, Father kicked to make the wheel spin until the lump of clay was just a whirling blur. He quickly cupped his slender hands around the clay and shaped it carefully into a graceful curved bowl.

Takao waited to speak until the bowl was finished. He loved to come to the workshop and squat down on the dirt floor beside Father, watching as he worked and speaking to him of many things. Sometimes Father would talk to him as though he were not just a child. Sometimes he would tell Takao of the little village beside the sea where he had lived when he was a boy. He would tell how his own father had also been a potter and taught him how to make beautiful shapes from clay. He would tell how poor they had been, and how they grew rice and wheat in the fields around their thatch-roofed house. Sometimes Father would rub his back, just remembering how he had bent to weed the rice paddies on long hot days.

"For you there will be no such struggle to grow food from a tired land," he said to Takao. "For you there will be only the struggle to make beautiful things on the potter's wheel." And then he would tell Takao how glad he was that he had left the old farm village so he could raise his own family in the city of Kyoto.

Father's face grew gentle as he worked with the clay, and Takao decided it was time to speak. "Father," he began, "wouldn't it be time now?"

Father knew what Takao meant, but he asked as though he didn't know.

"Time?" he asked, his lips curving into a smile. "Time for what?"

"You know," Takao said impatiently. "Time for me to learn. You said you would let me help you in the workshop soon."

"Ah, that," Father said. He took the bowl from the wheel now and placed it on the shelf behind him to dry. "It is not quite time yet," he said. "You are not quite ready."

Takao edged closer to his father. "But you said yourself it would be hard to make Kato-san's order all by yourself," he reminded him.

Father didn't answer, and began instead to speak of an entirely different matter. "Now what was it you said this morning when Mother found the charcoal box empty?"

Takao knew exactly what Father meant. Last night Mother had asked him to fill the charcoal box in the kitchen. "I'll need some in the morning to cook the rice," she had said. "You won't forget, will you?"

Takao had promised he wouldn't, but first there was the map of Japan he had to draw for class, and after that, he had to listen to the serial on the radio, and then, there was the last chapter to read in the book due at the library. He hadn't thought of the charcoal again until he heard Mother going outside for it this morning.

"I forgot all about the charcoal last night," Takao murmured to Father. "But working with you in the shop would be different. I wouldn't forget anything. I'd be careful. Honest I would!"

"And what was it that made your little sister cry the other day?" Father went on. "Was it about your pencil box?"

Takao remembered how he had scolded Sumi and made her cry because he thought she had taken his pencil box. And then, the next morning, he had found it on top of his desk at school. He had forgotten to put it in his schoolbag when he left for home.

Takao stood up now, his hands deep in his pockets, and kicked up little clouds of dirt with his toe. "Goro's father lets him help in his workshop," he said sullenly.

"Ah, but your friend Goro is a very reliable and dependable boy," Father said. "And older than you, too."

"Not much older," Takao murmured. "Only a couple of months."

He didn't like to admit it, but Goro actually did seem much older. He always seemed to do and say exactly the right things, and he never forgot the things he was supposed to do. Maybe it was because he wore those thick glasses!

Father looked up from his work and laughed softly. "Never mind, Takao," he said. "Someday you will be ready to help me. I shall know when you are, and then you will work here beside me. One day you will even have a wheel of your very own and you shall make pots even more beautiful than mine. I shall be very proud of you then."

Takao knew the conversation had come to an end. There was just no use saying anything more. He went out into the yard where Sumi was serving chopped camellia leaves on little tin plates to her friend from next door. She carefully poured a tiny cup of grass tea and then called to Takao. "Where are you going?" Sumi always wanted to know what he was going to do, and if she could, she would try to go along.

"Oh, some place," he answered vaguely. He wasn't sure himself just what he would do. Perhaps he would go see Goro and tell him about the big order from Mr. Kato.

He went into the house and saw that Mother had put on her apron again and wrapped a towel around her hair.

"Father and I will have to work hard," she murmured. "I do hope I wasn't wrong in promising to finish the tea sets by the first." She frowned as she looked at the calendar and counted the days still left in October.

"You could finish if you'd let me help," Takao murmured, but Mother scarcely listened to him.

"Don't stay too late at Goro's," she said, and she brushed past him as she hurried to the workshop.

It was amazing the things that Mother always knew. How had she known he was thinking of going to Goro's?

Takao stopped to look again at his *samurai* sword in the alcove. It wasn't often that he could look at it, for Mother usually kept it in a wooden box on the top shelf of the closet. She had taken it down just yesterday in honor of Grandfather's memorial day. Takao knelt at the alcove and gently lifted the sword from its wooden rack. He drew the sword carefully from its scabbard and inspected the strong shiny blade. Takao wondered how many enemy *samurai* had died by that sword. He looked around quickly to make sure no one watched, and then stood and raised the sword in the air.

"Kora! Yai! Yoisho!" he cried softly, bringing the sword down again and again. He cut down dozens of enemy *samurai* that surrounded him and had just raised his sword for one more blow when he heard Sumi shout to him.

"Taka-chan! Mother said you weren't to play with that sword!" She stood wide-eyed, watching him thrash the sword about in the air.

Takao quickly thrust the sword into its scabbard and then waved it threateningly at Sumi. "Don't you dare tell her you saw me," he warned. And then he ran to the entrance and slipped on his wooden clogs.

Takao ran all the way to Goro's house and got there panting and breathless. "Guess who came to our house today," he called as he went in, and as he heard Goro's answering shout, he wondered what Goro would say if he told him Father was going to let him help with the big order from Kato-san.

TWO

Goro Comes to Watch

When Takao told Goro about the twenty-five tea sets that Father would have to make in less than three weeks, Goro whistled through his teeth and pushed his glasses up on his nose. Goro had a habit of pushing up the bridge of his glasses with his forefinger, and Takao always thought this was something else that made him look older and more scholarly. Goro blinked now, as he multiplied figures in his head as quickly as though he had the beads of an abacus to help him.

"Twenty-five tea sets with five cups in each. That's one hundred and twenty-five cups and twenty-five teapots your father has to make," he said.

Takao blinked back at Goro and scratched his head. "I guess you're right," he murmured. "That sure is a lot of cups, isn't it?"

"And your father isn't going to let you help yet?" Goro asked, as though it were high time he did.

Goro's father was a dyer of silk, with a shop that faced the Kamo River. Since last year, he had let Goro deliver packages to his customers and he even let him come to the shop to wash out the brushes the men used for dyeing patterns into the long rolls of silk. And when the men took their afternoon break, Goro was permitted to stay and have tea with them and listen to their talk.

Even though Goro was one of his best friends, Takao felt a little jealous of him. Goro did so many things that he could not do. And whenever they did things together, Goro was always better. For instance, he could multiply faster, and he could read more of the new Japanese characters in their reader. He could write better with brush and ink, and he could even run faster. Just once, Takao always thought, he'd like to be able to do something Goro couldn't do.

"Well?" Goro asked now as he looked at Takao. "Isn't your father going to let you help with such a big order?"

Suddenly, Takao found himself saying, "Sure he is. That's what I came to tell you."

"What's he going to let you do?" Goro asked quickly.

"Well," Takao began, "he said . . . he said I could help stoke the fire in the kiln." This was the first thing that had come to his mind, although he knew very well that he wasn't permitted to touch anything near the kiln when it was being fired.

"Say, that'll be fun," Goro said eagerly. "Can I come watch?"

Takao gulped. Now he had done it. He couldn't possibly say no when Goro always let him go along to his father's shop. And he surely couldn't admit now that he had lied. There was nothing to do but to make another lie.

Takao took a deep breath and said bravely, "Sure, you can come. I might even let you help me."

Goro pushed up his glasses. "Will you really?" he asked. "Don't forget!"

"I won't," Takao said. "I'll let you know when Father's going to fire the kiln."

He managed to grin as he said good-by to Goro, but as he walked home, scuffling his heels in the dirt road, Takao knew he had begun something that promised nothing but trouble.

The next day was Grandfather's Memorial Day, and Mother bought the cakes of sweet bean paste and rice flour that Grandfather had liked so well. When Takao got home from school, he saw three cakes placed on a small dish in front of Grandfather's picture in the black and gold shrine. Takao grinned. If Mother had bought cakes for Grandfather, she had bought some for them too. And tomorrow, when Grandfather's spirit had finished with these three, he and Sumi would be permitted to have them. They would be a little hard, but Mother would toast them over charcoal until they were soft and puffy.

I will take two because I am older, Takao thought to himself, and I shall give one to Sumi-chan.

When Mother made three o'clock tea that day, even Father left his work to come inside. They all sat together at the low table and spoke of Grandfather as they ate their cakes and drank their cups of steaming green tea.

"Your grandfather was a fine man indeed," Father said to Takao. He glanced at the sword in the alcove and added, "Don't ever forget why he gave you that sword. He wanted you to be truthful and brave and loyal, just like his own *samurai* father who once wore that sword."

Takao winced. He nodded, but he kept his eyes on his sweet cake instead of looking up at Father. He hoped Grandfather's spirit had not heard his lie to Goro. If Father would only let him help with the firing, it wouldn't have to be a lie at all. Takao waited until the talk drifted once more to Father's work.

"If the weather continues to be kind," Mother

said hopefully, "I think some of the cups will be dry enough for the first firing in another day or two."

"And when will you do the last firing in the big kiln?" Takao asked quickly. "When will that be?"

Father held up his hands and shook his head. "I haven't even finished making all the pieces and already you talk of the final firing," he said. "You almost sound like our friend, Kato-san!"

"I just wondered," Takao began cautiously, "when you do fire the big kiln, could I just help you throw in a few pieces of kindling?"

"Me too," Sumi added immediately. "I want to help too. Can I, Father?"

Takao nudged her with his elbow. "You're not old enough," he said fiercely.

Father shook his head at both of them. "Fire is not a thing to be played with," he said gravely. "It has the power to make pottery, but it can also destroy. Before anything else, you must learn that fire is to be feared and respected."

"But I do respect it, Father," Takao objected. "I can help and still respect it. Honest!"

Now Mother shook her head. "It is best you do

not disturb your father this time," she said. "This is an important order, and we cannot have anything go wrong."

"Mother is right," Father agreed, and now he rose to return to the workshop. "Next time, perhaps," he added, "but not this firing."

Now, Takao could only hope that Goro would just forget about the whole thing. He was careful not to say anything more about Father's work, and when they walked home from school each day, he would talk instead of his insect collection, or of his new stamps, or of the baseball games at school.

The October days were clear and bright, and Takao knew that the work went well. He saw the yard crowded with cups and pots drying in the sun and knew it would soon be time for them to be fired in the big kiln.

Takao walked home from school with Goro one afternoon, full of silent, anxious thoughts. Somehow, he had a feeling Goro would ask about the firing of the kiln, and he wondered if he should confess and tell him he had lied about helping Father.

Fortunately, Goro had bought a bag of toasted chestnuts, and he didn't think it strange at all that

Takao should be so silent. They both knew chestnuts were easier to peel if you didn't talk, and of
course, once they were in your mouth, it was quite
impossible to say a word.

They had just turned the corner at the beancurd
shop when they both saw the big truck in front of
Takao's house. Takao gulped as he saw what the men
were unloading. They had brought the pine kindling for the firing of the kiln.

Goro's face brightened. "Say, it looks like your
father's finished his tea sets," he said eagerly.

"Uh-huh . . . looks like," Takao agreed glumly.

"Well," Goro went on, "when shall I come?
When will you fire the kiln?"

He hadn't forgotten after all. If Takao were to
save himself, this was his last chance. But when he
opened his mouth, he found himself saying, "I'll
ask Father. I'll let you know."

Goro paused at Takao's gate to watch the last of
the bundles being taken to the shed behind
Father's workshop, but Takao did not ask him to
come in. "See you tomorrow," he said, hoping Goro
would go on home.

But at that very moment, Father himself came
out to pay the men for the kindling. He nodded to

Goro and asked if his parents were well.

"Yes, thank you," Goro answered, and in almost the same breath he asked when Father would be firing the kiln. Goro did not waste time on useless talk.

"If all goes well," Father answered, "I think it will be on Saturday."

Takao groaned softly to himself. There was no school on Saturday afternoon. Nothing would keep Goro away.

From the very moment Takao opened his eyes on Saturday morning, he felt the strange shivery feeling of waiting for something. It was like waiting just before the test papers were passed out at school, or waiting for a balloon to burst into a piece of shredded rubber. Takao felt unhappy and anxious and did not hurry as he got up from his quilts.

Somehow the whole house seemed strangely silent. Takao could smell the freshly cooked rice and the bean soup, but there were no sounds at all coming from the kitchen. Even Sumi had gotten up early, and as Takao went to wash his face, he could hear Mother and Father already at work in the shed. Takao knew they must be stacking the pottery in the kiln, and he knew the firing would not be put off as he had hoped. It would take place today for sure.

Goro reminded him of it as they walked home from school. "I'll be over after lunch," he said, and Takao could only nod glumly.

Even the weather seemed unhappy and fretful, for the sky turned gray and a strong wind blew down from the mountains to the east.

"There's going to be a typhoon," Sumi said, looking at the sky.

But Takao scoffed at her. "Aw, don't be silly," he said. "The typhoon season ended in September!"

Still, the wind did make him feel uneasy, and he could tell that Mother didn't like it either

"It is not a good day for firing the kiln," she said. "We must be very watchful of sparks." She asked Father if he would not like to wait another day, but Father looked at the calendar and said there was no time.

When lunch was over, Mother put on her wool shawl and got her market basket from the hook in the kitchen. "Come along, Sumi-chan," she called. "There's fresh mackerel at the fish shop today, and I want to shop early so I can help Father later on."

Sumi was happy to have something to do. She put on her red sweater and ran quickly after Mother. Takao was glad they had left the house, for in just a little while, he heard Goro at the front entrance.

"Why aren't you out helping your Father?" Goro asked as soon as he came in. "Hasn't he begun yet?"

"Sure, he began this morning," Takao said feebly. "I was just waiting for you."

"Come on, then," Goro urged.

Takao went to get his towel, and rolling it into a narrow strip, he tied it around his head, just as Father did. "Father always says it's best to tie one's head firmly when there's a big job to do," Takao explained. But Goro did not seem interested at all. Already he moved toward the shed outside, calling, "Hurry up! Come on!"

Inside the shed, the great black kiln roared like a hollow mountain filled with flames, and Takao could see the bright orange glow at each of the small portholes along its sides.

Father scarcely noticed the two boys as they came in. He stood at the mouth of the kiln and tossed in the pine kindling one stick at a time. *"Yoisho!"* he sang out as he worked. *"Yoisho!"* At last, Takao cleared his throat and Father looked up.

"Did you boys want something?" he asked.

"I've . . . I've come to help you," Takao said in a small voice.

"*Yoisho!*" Father threw in another piece of wood. "What did you say?" he asked.

This time Goro spoke up quickly. "He's come to help and I've come to watch!" he shouted.

Father looked startled, and then he saw Takao's long sad face and the towel tied hopefully around his head. "Ah," he said slowly, "I see."

Takao knew then that Father really did see. He seemed to understand exactly what Takao had done. He was silent for a while, and then he said gently, "The firing goes well now, Takao. I think I can manage alone for the time being. Don't touch anything while I check the temperature."

Father moved quickly from one porthole of the kiln to the next, peering inside to see the color of the flame. "It's heating up nicely," he said, almost more to himself than to the boys, and then he went back to stoking the fire and he did not ask Takao to help.

Goro watched silently for a long while, and then he turned to Takao. "You sure are a big help!" he

said with a light laugh. "If you're just going to stand and watch, I may as well go home. Father might take me to Osaka with him."

Takao was about to stop him, but what was the use. Goro probably knew very well that Father had never meant to let him help.

"Go on, then," Takao said darkly, and he didn't even turn as Goro left the shed.

THREE

The Fire

Takao pulled the towel from his head and walked out dolefully into the yard. The wind was blowing in strange gusts now and sent the yellow gingko leaves from the tree next door whirling crazily into their yard. Takao kicked angrily at the ground and watched the wind pick up the dirt and whirl it away. Why had he told Goro he was helping Father, anyway! Goro hadn't been fooled at all. He had just laughed at him. Takao kicked angrily at the box Sumi had used for her tea table, scattering the small tin dishes in all directions.

"Stop it!" Sumi shouted. She had the most annoying way of appearing at just the wrong moment!

"Aw, I didn't do anything," Takao murmured.

"You did too," Sumi said, hurrying outside. "You kicked my dishes all over the yard." She bent quickly to gather them from the ground.

Takao felt mean and cross. "The wind did it," he

said. "If I did it, they'd go a lot farther. Look," he said, and he kicked the last dish, flinging it clear across the yard.

Sumi began to scream, and when Sumi screamed, she could make a small argument sound like a terrible calamity. *"Fa-ther!"* she wailed. "Make Takao stop! *Fa-ther!"*

Takao tried to stop her, but already Father hurried from the shed. "What happened?" he asked, looking alarmed. "Is Sumi-chan hurt?"

Sumi ran to him and sobbed out her story. "Takao is so mean to me," she cried.

Takao picked up the dish he had kicked and brought it back to Sumi. "What a big racket you make," he said, disgusted. "Stop crying. I'm sorry."

Father looked annoyed. "If you'd really like to help me," he said sternly to Takao, "you will behave while I am busy with the kiln." He turned to Sumi next and asked, "Where's Mother?"

Sumi gathered in the last sob that shivered through her body and explained that Mother had gone to the corner to buy some beancurd cakes.

"Well, see that you behave until she gets home," Father said firmly to both of them. "I don't want to be bothered again."

"*Hai*," Takao answered dismally. Now it was not just Goro, Father was annoyed with him too.

Father had just gone back to the shed when Takao heard his call for help. "Takao! Quickly!" he shouted. "Get some water!" His voice was urgent, and Takao raced to the shed. He gasped as he looked in and saw flames blazing, not just inside the kiln where they belonged, but outside around the mouth of the kiln. All the kindling had caught on fire!

"Hurry, Takao!" Father shouted. "I'll try to smother it with dirt!"

While Father shoveled dirt on the blaze, Takao ran to the workshop for water. He staggered back to the shed with two full buckets, but when Father flung them on the fire, it only hissed and sizzled and filled the shed with a billowing cloud of smoke. The smoke stung at Takao's eyes and seeped into his lungs. He began to cough, and Father shouted hoarsely, "Go get help, Takao. It's getting too big for us."

If we only had a telephone, Takao thought frantically. The closest one was at the beancurd shop. Takao raced out of the house without even putting on his *geta* and caught up with Sumi already run-

ning up the street calling for Mother. They both
ran into her coming down the street with her market basket full of food, and they shouted at her in a
jumble of confused words.

"Fire!" Sumi shrieked.

"The kindling's on fire!" Takao shouted, and
then, without even giving Mother a chance to say
a word, he ran on to the corner. He reached the
beancurd shop panting and breathless.

"Fire!" he shouted in such a loud voice, the old
man dropped his scoop into the tub of boiling
water.

"Now, see what you made me do," he said
crossly. "Don't frighten me like that."

"But our kindling's on fire," Takao shouted.
"Call the fire engine! Hurry!"

The old man saw that Takao was not joking.
"Your father's kindling?" he asked, and this time
he dropped the scoop on the floor and ran to his
telephone to call the fire department.

"Hurry," Takao begged, and then he could not
bear to wait. He ran back again toward home and
saw that the street was filled now with people who
had heard the shouts and smelled the smoke. Men
were coming from all directions with shovels and

buckets and old tubs. They knew that if one house caught fire, all their houses of paper and wood were in danger too.

Takao tried to get to the shed, but the men all pushed him back. "This is no place for children," they said, and they sent him out into the street.

"I want to help! It's my father's shed!" Takao said, but no one paid any attention to him.

The men sent Mother outside too, with Sumi weeping and clinging to her *kimono*. She stood pale and frightened and silent, watching the smoke drift higher into the sky.

Now, Takao heard the whine of the fire engine and the clanging of its bells as it tried to clear people from its path. It had to come slowly, for there was barely room for it to pass down the narrow street. The firemen leaped from the truck and ran to the shed with their hose and hatchets.

Takao tried to follow the last fireman into the shed, but he was quickly pushed outside. "This is no place for you," the fireman said firmly, and he cleared out all the men who had come to help.

"Stay out of our way, please," he shouted, but when he tried to get Father to leave, Father would not move.

"It is my shed," he said firmly. "I will stay to help save it."

The air was thick with smoke now, and people edged away from the house, coughing and rubbing their eyes. The women clustered about Mother, flapping their aprons to drive away the smoke, and trying to find words to comfort her. "Such a terrible thing," they murmured sympathetically. "But

the firemen will surely save your house."

"The workshop and the kiln . . . my husband's work . . . they are almost more important than the house," Mother said miserably.

Gradually, the smoke began to die away, and slowly the firemen returned to their truck, wiping their faces with their sleeves.

"We caught it just in time," the chief said to

Mother. "Your house is safe, but most of the shed is gone."

"And the kiln?" Mother asked almost in a whisper. "Is it all right?"

"It still stands," the chief answered. "It was built to hold fire just as hot as the one we put out, but I'm afraid the fire inside it is gone. We put out every spark in that whole shed."

"Then the tea sets inside are ruined," Mother said sadly. "Kato-san's order gone . . . after all that hard work."

When Takao saw that no one would stop him, he ran into the house and hurried to the workshop. Half the walls had been burned away, and the dirt floor was a soggy mass of mud. Buckets of glaze had been knocked over and spilled, and even Father's wheel lay on its side looking like an injured and helpless animal. It was as though a typhoon and earthquake had struck all at once.

Takao hurried to the shed and saw that there was nothing left of it but its tin roof and a few charred supports. The kiln was still there, but now it was dark and black. No warm lights glowed from any of the portholes along its sides, but still Father walked around and looked inside at each one.

"Father," Takao called, but Father did not answer. His face was white and his lips were pressed together in a grim line.

"Are the tea sets spoiled?" Takao asked anxiously.

"I'm not sure," Father answered. "The kiln is still too hot to open." He sighed deeply and shook his head. "If only I had not left it," he said over and over again, and he didn't seem to hear anything else that Takao said to him.

Now Mother hurried in with Sumi and the fire chief close behind.

"How did it begin, Sakata-san?" the chief asked Father.

"It was the wind," Father said dismally. "I left the kiln for just a moment . . . the children were quarreling and I went outside to see. The wind must have blown sparks from the fire chamber onto the kindling. It was so dry it took only a second for it to burst into flames."

The chief shook his head. "It is too bad," he said slowly. "Too bad indeed."

"It was not a good day for the firing," Mother said sadly. "And I should not have left to go marketing. If only I had been here to help."

"I was foolish to leave the kiln even for a moment

on such a windy day," Father said miserably.

Takao didn't want to hear any more. Both Mother and Father were blaming themselves, when it had really been his fault. If he hadn't teased Sumi and made her cry, Father never would have left the kiln. He had just proved once more that he wasn't dependable at all. Father would probably never forget this, and now he would never let him help with his work. Takao went back into the house, but it was still full of the smell of smoke. It stung at his throat and it prickled at his eyes, but Takao knew that the tears he rubbed back were not just from the smoke.

It all seemed like a horrible nightmare, and that night when Takao crept into his quilts, he discovered that their troubles had only begun. He closed his eyes and tried to sleep, but over and over, he saw the billowing smoke and heard the anxious shouts, and more than anything else, he saw the sadness in Father's face.

Takao could hear Mother and Father talking in the next room, and he lay quietly, his toes curled tight, trying to hear what they said.

"If only I had not left the kiln," Father was saying once again. "Now the shed is gone, the work-shop in ruins, and the kindling gone up in smoke."

"And what shall we say to Kato-san?" Mother added in a worried voice. "He will be so terribly angry."

"Not only will he be angry," Father said dis-mally, "he will probably never bring me another order again. And now, there isn't money enough even to buy more kindling. How shall I save the tea sets left in the kiln?"

There was a long silence now, as though each of them was burdened with thoughts too terrible to put into words.

At last, Mother spoke so softly Takao could scarcely hear what she said. "I could sell my wed-ding *kimono* and my gold brocade sash," she said. "And then, there are the tortoise shell combs my mother gave me."

Father sighed deeply. "I do not wish you to sell those things that mean much to you," he said. "Surely, there must be another way."

Takao had never heard Mother and Father talk of selling their things before. He knew now what a terrible thing the fire had been, and he knew too that somehow he must help make things right again.

Takao turned over on his quilt and thought of the things he might sell to help make some money. There were his baseball and his catcher's mitt—his birthday presents for the last two years. And then, there was the pocket knife from his uncle in Tokyo, with the bone handle and four beautiful blades. But these were only small things. If only he had something so wonderful and so valuable it would bring a tremendous sum of money and solve all of Father's problems at once!

And then, suddenly, it came to him. Takao remembered how Mr. Kato had looked at Grandfather's sword and said he would pay a good sum for it. Selling the sword would surely help Father, but how could he possibly sell it to that horrible Mr. Kato? Takao didn't even want to think of such a terrible thing. He shuddered at the thought, and as he tried hard to think of another way to help Father, he finally fell asleep.

But in his sleep he had a dream. He was wandering about in a great dark forest, clutching Grandfather's sword and searching for the path that would lead him home. In the darkness, he stumbled on a big moss-covered log, but it was not a log at all. It was a dragon with a great thorny tail and five pair of legs. The dragon wore a pair

of round black glasses and from its mouth came a
hissing cloud of fire and smoke.

The dragon slithered toward him shouting, "Ha,
so the little one with the loud tongue comes creeping to me now for money, does he? Very well, then,
give me the sword! Give me the sword!"

Takao clung to the sword and began to run.
"No!" he shouted. "I won't let you have it! It's
mine!"

The dragon had just reached out for it with a

great horny claw when Takao heard a man calling from the shadows of the forest. "Give it to me, Takao. I will keep it safely for you." Was it Father's voice? Or Grandfather's? Takao tossed the sword in the direction of the friendly voice just as the dragon reached for it again.

"There! Now you won't get it," Takao cried, and it was his own shout that awakened him. Takao opened his eyes to the silent darkness of his room.

"Whew," he sighed, "it was only a dream!" His hands were clammy, and he shivered at the narrow escape he had just had.

Who was it that had called to him from the shadows of the forest? Who had come just in time to help him?

Takao thought again of the sword, and then, slowly, he knew what he could do. He didn't have to sell it to Mr. Kato at all. If the sword was so valuable, there must be other people who would want to buy it too. Perhaps, he could take it to one of the antique and curio shops on Temple Street. Or, better still, perhaps he could take it to Father's friend, Mr. Mori. He owned just such a shop, and surely he would give him a good sum for the sword. Maybe the friendly voice in the forest had belonged to Mori-san.

Takao felt sad to think of selling Grandfather's sword. It was the only real treasure he had ever owned, and no one in all of Kinrin School—not even Goro—had anything like it. Still, helping Father was more important now, and Takao knew he had to show that, for once, he could really be helpful.

Tomorrow was Sunday and there was no school. He would get up early and take the sword alone so he could surprise Father later on. He grinned as he thought how pleased Father would be, and soon he fell asleep and dreamed no more.

FOUR

The Shop Behind the Mailbox

The big brown clock on the wall ticked away the minutes of the sunny Sunday morning. Takao opened one eye and looked at it sleepily. Only eight o'clock and no school today! Maybe he would go kite-flying with Goro in the afternoon. But I'm mad at Goro, Takao thought suddenly. And then, he remembered the kiln and the fire, and most important, he remembered what he was going to do that morning. He listened a moment. The house was quiet, and Sumi was still huddled down in the middle of her quilts. Mother and Father were already working outside, and Takao knew they would be busy most of the day, cleaning up in the workshop and the shed.

He hurried to the closet and looked at the top shelf. The box was there, all right, just where Mother had put it. He took two of Father's big dictionaries and stood on them to reach it. Then he opened the box quickly and took one more look at the sword. He wondered if there wasn't something else he could sell instead, but when he thought of the big sum this would bring, he quickly wrapped the box in one of Mother's *furoshiki* and hid it between his quilts until he was ready to go.

Takao filled his rice bowl and took one bite of pickled radish when he heard Sumi stir in her quilts. He leaped up from the table. It would be better to skip breakfast than to have Sumi discover what he was up to. She'd want to go along for sure, and that was the last thing he wanted. Takao snatched the sword from his quilts, left his breakfast uneaten on the table, and ran out of the house as fast as he could go.

He turned the corner so he wouldn't have to pass Goro's house. Somehow, he didn't feel like telling Goro what had happened—at least, not just yet. He ran to the edge of the Kamo River and followed the road beside it, running beneath the trailing branches of the willow trees. He ran until his chest hurt from breathing so hard, and then he walked a while until he could run again. He crossed the river at the Nijo Bridge and then hurried on to Temple street, lined on both sides with rows and rows of antique and curio shops.

Takao knew Mr. Mori had a shop somewhere on
this street, but he had no idea just where it was.
He wandered from shop to shop, looking in at the
windows crowded with old iron kettles, and lacquer
bowls, and teacups and plates of fine old porcelain.
Surely, someone in one of these shops would know
where he could find Mr. Mori.

When he had gone halfway down the block, he
came to a beautiful shop much larger and cleaner
than all the rest. Somehow, Takao had the feeling
that this was Mori-san's shop. He walked in quickly
and saw a woman in a green *kimono* dusting the
shelves.

"Hai?" she said. "What can I do for you?" Her
face was caked with white powder, and she smelled
faintly of camellia hair oil.

"I'm looking for Mori-san's shop," Takao began.
"I thought this must be it, because it is so clean and
beautiful."

The woman threw back her head and laughed in
a high bubbling voice. "So it is Mori-san's shop
you want, is it?" She laughed again and came closer
to Takao. "Well, you couldn't have been more mis-
taken. Come here, little one," she said. "I'll show
it to you."

She plucked a corner of Takao's sleeve and pulled him to the front of the shop. "Look," she said, pointing down the street. "Do you see the red mailbox?" Takao nodded.

"Mori-san's shop is the one right behind it. You'll see it when you get there."

Takao bowed his thanks and hurried away. The woman still laughed as she watched him go, and when Takao reached the mailbox, he knew why. The shop just behind it was the smallest, shabbiest one on the whole block. Its windows were a jumble of junk, filled with everything from old coal stoves to chipped cups, suits of armor, and cracked *hibachi* that could never again hold glowing charcoal. Could this miserable old shop belong to Mori-san? Takao peered through the glass of the door and saw a plump, bald-headed man seated in a small *tatami*-matted room at the back of the shop. He was reading a book and sipping a cup of tea. It looked like Mori-san, all right. Takao opened the door and heard the tinkle of a rusty old bell above his head.

The round-faced man looked up and squinted through his cloudy glasses. "*Hai . . . hai.* Good morning. What can I do for you today?" he asked. He adjusted his glasses and looked carefully at

Takao. "Why, aren't you the son of Sakata-san, the potter?" he asked.

Takao nodded. "Yes, I am," he answered. And suddenly, he felt so tired and hungry, he sat down on the *tatami* beside Mori-san and could have eaten three bowls of rice right then and there.

"Well, it is nice to see you again," Mr. Mori said, smiling. "But what brings you here all alone on a Sunday morning? What can I do for you?"

"I think I'd like a cup of tea first of all," Takao said, looking longingly at Mr. Mori's pot of tea.

Mori-san raised both hands in the air. "Ah yes, how very rude of me," he said. "Of course you shall have a cup of tea. And would you like some salt rice crackers to go with it?"

Takao nodded. "Yes, please," he said eagerly. "I haven't had any breakfast."

Mori-san was startled. "No breakfast?" he said. "And you walked all the way from home?"

Takao shook his head. "No," he explained, "I ran all the way!"

Mr. Mori clucked sympathetically. He reached on the shelf behind him for a large black tin of rice crackers and a shallow green bowl beside it. He blew the dust from the bowl and then filled it with a fistful of rice crackers from the tin.

"*Sah . . . sah.* Eat! Eat!" he said, pushing the bowl toward Takao. "It is not the best breakfast I could suggest, but it will fill your stomach."

Takao ate eagerly and thought he had never tasted such delicious rice crackers in all his life.

Mori-san leaned on a small armrest padded with green velours and watched as Takao ate. After a moment, he bent forward and said, "Now tell me. Surely you did not come all the way to see me just to have a cup of tea."

He lowered his voice to a whisper and said softly, "Have you done something you shouldn't? And what is that package in your *furoshiki?*"

"This is Grandfather's sword," Takao began, after he had sipped the last drop of his tea. "He gave it to me, but now I want to sell it for a great sum of money."

"Ah . . . so?" Mori-san raised an eyebrow. "And with the money, what is it you hope to do?" he asked.

"I want to help Father buy some kindling," Takao explained, "and fix his workshop and his shed." Then, quickly, he told Mr. Mori all about the fire and the tea sets for Mr. Kato that had been spoiled and sat half-finished in the kiln.

Mori-san rubbed his forehead. "A fire is a bad thing anywhere," he said, "but in a potter's shed, it is a real tragedy." He shook his head just at the thought of it.

"Well, let me see this sword you want to sell," he said, and taking it from Takao, he examined it carefully.

"It looks like a fine sword," he said. "I think it might be worth a good sum of money, but I am not sure." He held the sword in his hands for a while and then he said slowly, "I think I shall send you to see a friend of mine."

Takao was disappointed. "Then, aren't you going to buy it from me?" he asked.

"No . . . no, don't you see?" Mr. Mori said, "I am not sure how valuable it really is. I am going to send you to see Yamaka-san. He is a great collector of old swords and porcelains. He will know the sword's value and he will give you a good price for it."

Mr. Mori took his letter-writing box from the shelf.

"I shall send you to him with a letter," he said, and dropping some water onto his *suzuri* stone, he rubbed with an ink stick until he had a small pool

of black ink. He chose a slim brush with a bamboo
handle, and then he wrote his letter on a long roll
of soft white paper.

Takao watched the paper unroll slowly, as Mori-
san filled it with rows and rows of dancing black
letters. It was the longest letter Takao had ever
seen.

When Mori-san finished, he folded the letter
over and over and slipped it into a long narrow
envelope.

"Now," he said, "do you know the Nanzenji
Temple?"

Takao nodded. "We've gone there from school
lots of times to sketch," he said.

"Ah, good. Then you know the house behind the
temple?" Mr. Mori asked. "The one with the high
white wall, just beyond the bamboo grove?"

"You mean the one where the crazy old man
lives?" Takao asked in alarm. "The house where the
night shutters are closed all day?"

"That is the house," Mr. Mori said, nodding. "But
don't be afraid. Yamaka-san is not crazy at all. You'll
see. He is just a little strange . . . and very sad."

"But . . . but . . . is that where you want me
to go?" Takao stammered.

Everyone knew about the strange old man who lived in the darkness and never came out in the light of day. Goro had told him that he lived on nothing but broiled snakes' tongues!

"He is a little peculiar, but he is honest and he can afford a good price," Mori-san explained. "I've already written the letter. *Sah, sah* . . . now go along, won't you?"

There was nothing for Takao to do but to nod and say yes. "I'll go, then," he said, and he thanked Mr. Mori and walked slowly in the direction of the temple.

Maybe I should go home and tell Father everything, Takao thought. Perhaps Father would go to see the old man with him. Takao stopped at the corner, wondering what he should do. But if he did not go now, how could he ever prove that he could help Father all by himself? Takao took a deep breath and decided he would go alone.

He wished now that he'd asked Goro to come along. At least Goro would have known what to say to Mr. Yamaka, and it would have been nice to have some company. Takao swallowed and felt his heart beating faster. Aw, I'm not afraid of that old man, he said to himself, but the closer he got to the shuttered house, the slower his steps became.

Soon he came to the big brown gate of the Nanzenji Temple. He glanced up at the broad curved
roof of the temple and decided it wouldn't hurt to
have a little help from Buddha or the priest or
whoever else would be inclined to give it to him.

Takao left the path and walked toward the
temple, weaving in and out among the tall pine
trees that stretched up to the sky. The ground was
covered with their soft brown needles, and Takao
padded along soundlessly. He climbed the flight of
stone steps, and as he got closer to the temple, he
heard the shivery sound of a brass gong and the
strange eerie voice of a priest chanting the sutra.

Takao shivered. He had gone often to the shrine
near his house, to clap and bow his head, but he
hadn't been to a temple since the day of Grandfather's funeral. Somehow, temples made him think
of ghostly ancestors asleep in their moss-covered
tombstones in the cemetery near by.

Suddenly, the chanting and the gongs stopped.
A door to the side of the temple slid open noiselessly, and a priest strode out onto the polished ve-
randa. His head was shaven, and he walked silently
in his snow-white *tabi,* wearing a robe of rustling

black silk. Takao heard only the faint click of his prayer beads as he approached.

Had he come out to scold Takao for snooping around the temple? Takao didn't wait to find out. He clapped his hands together and bowed as he had seen Mother do.

"Namu Amida Butsu!" he shouted at the priest, and then, turning, he ran as fast as he could toward the pine woods. He thought he heard the priest laugh softly, but he didn't stop to look back, and he ran until he had reached the graveled path once more. Then, he took a long deep breath.

At least now, he had Buddha on his side, and feeling a little better, Takao walked up the path that led to the house beyond the temple.

FIVE

The Shuttered House

Takao could see the thicket of soft green bamboo just ahead, and then he saw the high white wall that surrounded the shuttered house. He followed the wall until he came to the main gate. It was shut tight to keep out beggars and peddlers and burglars, and on the post there hung a wooden plaque with Mr. Yamaka's name written on it in bold black letters.

To the side of the gate was a small doorway with a white bell. Takao took a deep breath and rang the bell. He waited and listened, but there was no sound. Perhaps the old man never answered the bell. Takao rang once more, pushing a little harder this time.

Soon he heard the sound of *geta* scraping over the walk, and then a young girl's voice called out, "*Hai?* Who is it?"

Takao cleared his throat. "My name is Sakata,

Takao," he said in a loud voice, and he found himself bowing to the closed door.

"What is your business?" the voice asked next.

How could he tell what his business was? He couldn't shout the whole story of the fire and Mr. Mori and the sword to the person behind the door. And besides, he didn't like talking to a voice without seeing the body it came from. Then, he remembered the letter.

"I have a letter for Yamaka-san," he said quickly.

"Then you will kindly drop it in the letter box and depart," the voice answered.

Takao scratched his head. Now, what was he to do? If he dropped the letter into the box, perhaps Mr. Yamaka would never read it.

"Well . . . then, what shall I do with the sword?" he asked helplessly.

Suddenly, as though "sword" had been the magic password, the small door opened and a young girl of about sixteen peered out at Takao. She wore an apron over her flowered *kimono,* and her face was pale and thin.

"The master is always interested in swords," she said, glancing at the package under Takao's arm.

"Why didn't you say you had a sword in the first place?"

"You didn't ask me," Takao answered simply.

The young girl frowned. *"Mah,"* she said haughtily, "you are a stupid one! Come with me." And she motioned Takao to follow her to the house. She locked the door behind them and walked quickly toward the rear service entrance.

As Takao followed her, he saw that all the wooden night shutters were indeed closed. Then, all the stories he had heard about the old man were really true! He stopped to peek through the bamboo fence that enclosed an inner garden and had a quick glimpse of a beautiful curved pond with red maples bending over the water's edge.

"Well? Are you coming?" the young girl asked. "Hurry along. I'm very busy. It is almost time for the master's lunch."

Takao hurried. He removed his shoes at the rear entrance and shivered as he put on the pair of big cold leather slippers the girl had left for him. She frowned again as she saw his dusty bare feet, and Takao pushed his toes into the slippers to hide as much of his feet as he possibly could.

The girl pointed to a stool. "Sit down there and

wait," she commanded. And then, putting out her hand she said, "Now, let me have it."

Takao drew away from her. "No, I'll take the sword to him myself," he said.

The young girl clucked her tongue at him. "Not your sword, silly. I want the letter. Give it to me."

Takao took the letter from his pocket and grinned sheepishly. "You can have that, all right," he said.

The girl started down the dark hallway and then came back for a last word. "Now, don't you touch a single thing while I'm gone," she warned.

Takao nodded and then looked about the kitchen to see what had made her say that. On the table he saw the black lacquer tray on which she had been preparing the old man's lunch. There was a dish with slivers of fresh tuna arranged neatly on shavings of long white radish. Beside it was a small saucer of sweet lima beans, and then there was a dish of vinegared cucumbers with slices of fresh mushroom. She had left space on the tray for the bowl of rice and a bowl of the clear hot broth that simmered on the gas stove. There was nothing anywhere that looked like broiled snakes' tongues!

Takao swallowed hard and slipped slowly from the stool. Surely the old man wouldn't miss just one little slice of tuna if he could lift it off carefully. He stood for a moment in front of the tray, but as he looked at the feast before him, he heard again the voice of the young girl. She had told him not to touch a thing. Takao went quickly back to the stool and sat down, turning his head away so he would not see the food. It was best to do as he was told in this strange house! And now, he heard again the young girl's footsteps coming down the hall.

"*Sah,*" she said. "You will please follow me. The master will see you for a few minutes."

Takao clutched the sword tightly and followed the maid down the long dark hall. She glided noiselessly, moving as lightly and quickly as a small white mouse. Takao tried to keep up with her, but the slippers were so big and slippery, he had to drag them along so he would not walk right out of them.

Slap-slap . . . slap-slap . . . Takao flapped after her in his big slippers.

The girl turned and put a hand to her lips. "*Mah,* you make so much noise," she said in a loud whisper. "The master does not like noise at all."

It was impossible to walk quietly in those big slippers. Takao finally took them off, picked them up, and ran barefooted after her. The floor was as smooth and cold as a sheet of glass, and Takao shivered as he ran on his toes.

Now the maid stopped before a door. She knelt to the floor, slid open the paper doors, and then bowed.

"This is the child with the sword," she said, and she prodded Takao into the room.

The room was so dark, he could scarcely see, but he knew there was a shadowy figure sitting near the alcove. Takao quickly knelt to the *tatami* and bowed in that direction. When he looked up, the old gentleman snapped on a small light, and Takao saw how old he was. His face was pale and quite wrinkled, as though he might have been made of wads of rice paper. His narrow eyes were half-closed as he peered at Takao, and he stroked a white beard that trickled to his chest. It was just about as thin as the white hair on top of his head.

The old man motioned Takao to sit on the cushion opposite him. Takao was careful to sit properly with his legs tucked neatly beneath him.

He took a deep breath and waited anxiously for the old man to speak.

The old man continued to stare silently, and Takao began to wish he had never come. He did not look crazy, Takao thought, but there was something so strange and weird about the whole house. Takao glanced around the room and saw that it was quite bare, except for the small desk beside the brazier. He smelled incense and saw a thin trail of smoke drifting from a small container placed before the photograph of an old woman in the alcove.

"Name?" the old man said suddenly, in a surprisingly high voice.

"Sakata, Takao." He bowed once more as he answered.

"So it says in the letter," the old man said abruptly. "I wanted to know if you had a tongue with which to speak. Now, let me see this sword of yours."

Takao fumbled as he hurriedly unwrapped the box from his *furoshiki,* and he pushed it quickly toward the old man. Mr. Yamaka lifted the sword from the box and examined it even more carefully than Mr. Mori.

"Ah . . ." he said, squinting at it through his glasses. "Hmmmm. So . . ."

Takao wiggled on his cushion. Would the old man never speak? "Will you . . . would you . . . buy it from me?" he asked anxiously.

The old man paid no attention to him, and now he read Mr. Mori's letter once more. "So, your father is a potter, is he?" he asked.

Takao nodded and began to tell him about the fire, but the old man stopped him. "I know," he said. "It is all written in the letter."

"Then, will you really give me a big sum for the sword?" Takao asked. "Like Mori-san said?"

The old man suddenly reached over and snapped off the light.

"I think better in the dark," he said. "It is much more peaceful, and I find the light irritating."

Takao shrank back in alarm and felt cold shivers run down his back. The old man was crazy after all! He never should have come all alone and let the old man trap him in his dark house. He never should have listened to Mr. Mori!

Takao decided he would try to escape while the lights were still out, but he would have to take the sword with him. Slowly, slowly, he reached out and felt for the sword box. He pulled it toward him gently, and then, sliding quietly from his cushion, he began to creep toward the door. If he could just reach the door safely, he'd run down the hall and be out of the house before the old man knew what had happened. If he could just get there before the old man put on the lights once more.

Takao crept as softly as he could. He had almost reached the door when the old man spoke in a quiet, calm voice.

"Is it your custom to crawl about on your hands and knees? You know, I am used to the dark and I see you quite well."

Takao gulped. "No . . . that is, I . . . well . . . I think maybe I've made a mistake," he stammered. "I think I'll leave now."

"Ah, you find me a little peculiar, do you?" the old man asked.

"Yes," Takao answered. "I mean . . . that is . . ."

"That is natural," Mr. Yamaka said. "You are honest and that is good." He snapped on the light and then said, "Give me your sword. I shall buy it from you for 8000 *yen*."

Takao was not sure how much kindling and lumber that would buy, but he was anxious to take what he could and leave. He watched as the old man reached into the folds of his *kimono* and drew out a worn wallet. He counted out eight 1000 *yen* notes and handed them to Takao.

"*Sah*," he said. "This is to help you help your father. And bring him to see me sometime. I might be able to help him in still another way."

Takao took a deep breath and managed to smile at last. The old man was not so bad when you got used to him. "Thank you," he said, bowing. "I'll tell Father. I'll bring him for sure. I promise."

The old man nodded. "Very well," he said. "See that you do." He waved a thin hand in the air to indicate that Takao might leave. "And now," he said briefly, "it is time for my lunch."

"*Hai*. Thank you. *Sayonara*," Takao murmured, and he hurried out of the room before the old man could turn out the lights again. He flapped his way noisily to the kitchen and found the young girl sitting on the stool waiting for him.

"*Mah*, you stayed a long time," she complained. "The soup has nearly boiled itself away."

"I'm sorry. I couldn't help it," Takao said. "The old man . . . I mean, the master had to turn out the lights and think."

He slipped quickly into his shoes and started toward the gate without even bothering to tie his laces. The young girl hurried after him to lock the door, and as Takao heard the click behind him, he took a deep breath of the fresh sunny air and began to run. He felt as though he had been freed from a dark tomb!

And he had 8000 *yen!* That was more money than he had ever seen all at once. The wad of money in his pocket felt as big as a baseball, and Takao felt as though everyone on the street knew how much he was carrying. He would have to be careful of pickpockets and act as though nothing unusual had happened.

Takao slowed down and tried to whistle, but nothing would come from his lips but a weak little squeak. He couldn't wait to see Father's face when he gave him the money, and at last, Takao began to run once more. How could he act as though nothing had happened when he'd just had the most exciting morning of his whole life!

SIX

Takao's Big Surprise

When Takao finally got home, he found the house in an uproar. The men from the neighborhood had come to help Father repair the workshop and shed, and the yard was filled with sounds of hammering and sawing and the urgent voices of the workers. Mother was in the kitchen making a big pan of hot noodles to serve the men for lunch, and Sumi was helping her line up the big bowls on a large wooden tray.

"Mother!" Takao shouted as he ran into the house. "Guess what I just did!"

But Sumi called to him before Mother could answer. "Where've you been all morning anyway? I looked every place for you!"

"*Mah,* Takao," Mother added, "as though I didn't have enough to do without worrying about you." She seemed tired and annoyed as she pushed back a wisp of hair that had slipped from the towel around her head. "You didn't even finish your breakfast!"

"But Mother," Takao began, "I've been to . . ."

Before he could go any further, there was a loud voice at the front entrance. *"Kon nichi wa.* Is anybody home?"

Mother grew pale. "That sounds like Mr. Kato," she whispered. "What shall we say to him? Taka-chan, go call your father. Quickly!"

"But Mother, I . . ." Takao tried to tell his story, but Mother would not listen.

"Quickly!" she urged. "Hurry!"

Takao ran outside to tell Father that Mr. Kato had come. Father had been so busy working, he didn't even seem to know that Takao had been gone all morning.

"Ah, so he has come," he said simply, and brushing the dirt from his clothes, he hurried inside.

Mr. Kato had already removed his shoes and stepped inside.

"Good morning," Father said. He bowed, but Mr. Kato did not bother to return it.

"What is this I hear about a fire?" he asked brusquely.

"Unfortunately, it is true," Father answered sadly. "It was a bad day to fire the kiln. My shed is gone and the workshop in ruins."

"And my tea sets?" Mr. Kato pressed. "What of

them? Tomorrow is the first of November, and you promised.''

Father shook his head. "It is impossible to finish them now," he explained. "The firemen put out the fire in the kiln, as well as the flames outside. The tea sets are only half-finished, and I have no money to buy more kindling."

Takao tried to tell Father that he could help him. "Father," he began. "Father, I can help . . ."

But Father would not listen. "Not now, Takao," he said firmly, and Takao knew he would just have to wait until Mr. Kato left.

"We are so very sorry," Mother said to Mr. Kato. "It was an unfortunate accident, but there is nothing we can do."

Takao thought Mr. Kato would explode with anger. He clenched his fists and grew red in the face and began to shout angrily.

"But you promised! You had no right to fail me like this. What will I say to my customer? I will lose a great sum of money. I will be ruined!" he shouted. "Let me see what you have done to my tea sets. Open the kiln at once!"

Before Father could stop him, Mr. Kato stormed out toward the kiln, pushing aside the men who were helping Father in the workshop.

Father followed, with Takao close behind. "The kiln is still hot," Father explained. "I do not think it would be wise to open it yet."

But Mr. Kato would not listen. "Open it immediately," he demanded. "I insist upon it."

Father pulled on a pair of heavy gloves. "Very well," he said slowly. "If that is what you wish."

He pulled away some bricks to open up the kiln, and then reached in and brought out one of the teapots. It was a strange dull gray instead of the clear green it should have been. The pot still snapped from the heat as Father brought it out into the cold air, and Takao was surprised to see him hand it to Mr. Kato. "Would you care to examine it yourself?" he asked.

Mr. Kato took the pot in his hands and then shouted in such a loud voice everyone came to see what had happened.

"*Atsui! Atsui!* It's hot!" he cried. He juggled the pot back and forth from one hand to another and finally thrust it helplessly at Father.

Takao couldn't help laughing as he watched, and even the men who had stopped their work threw back their heads and laughed out loud.

Now, Mr. Kato was so angry, he could scarcely speak. "Fool!" he shouted at Father. "I will never

forget this. You will never get another order from me, and I shall see that none of the shops on Gojo Hill ever buys another pot from you again. Just see how far you can get without my help!"

Still fuming angrily, Mr. Kato stamped out through the house.

Mother gasped and followed him to the entrance. "I am sure my husband meant no offense," she called after him. "He did not mean to anger you, Kato-san."

But Father stopped her. "Let him go," he said wearily. "Let him go. I have had all I can stand of him."

"*Yah,* that's the end of the cranky old dragon," Takao said gleefully.

But Father did not seem happy at all. "More likely it is the end of me," he said. "Kato-san is a powerful figure. He might very well be able to keep me from selling my pottery to any of the shops on Gojo Hill."

"What will we do if no one will buy your pottery?" Mother asked anxiously. "Perhaps I should go apologize to Kato-san. Perhaps he will lend us money so we can finish the tea sets."

Takao was about to explode from wanting to tell

about the sword, and now he could wait no longer.

"Mother! Father! Look!" he shouted, taking the money from his pocket and thrusting it at Father. "I've got 8000 *yen!* I can help you buy kindling. I can help you fix the shed. You don't have to borrow from that old Kato-san!"

"Takao! But where . . . how . . . what did you do?" Father gasped.

"*Mah,* Taka-chan," Mother said. She looked worried and alarmed.

"Where'd you get it?" Sumi asked. "What did you do?"

Everyone began to talk all at once, but Takao's voice was the loudest of all. "I sold my sword," he burst out. "I sold it to the old man in the shuttered house!"

"You mean, you went to that spooky house behind the temple all by yourself?" Sumi asked wonderingly.

"Sure I did," Takao said grandly, and now he poured out the whole long story of what he had done. He told how Mori-san had sent him with the letter; he told about the strange young maid; and he told how Yamaka-san had turned out the lights and then finally given him 8000 *yen* for the sword.

Father seemed too surprised even to speak. "Did you really sell your sword?" he asked, as though he could not believe it. "Grandfather's *samurai* sword?"

Takao grinned. Father looked exactly as surprised as he thought he would. "I wanted to show you I could help too," he said. And he felt as proud then, as though he had just climbed to the top of Mt. Fuji.

Father blinked and looked as though he had many words he would like to say, but when he tried to speak, all he could say was, "I know the sword meant much to you, Takao. I am grateful."

It was the first time since the fire that Takao saw Father smile.

"Is that enough money to build a new shed and fix the workshop too?" Takao asked anxiously.

Mother's voice was gentle as she answered. "The amount doesn't matter," she said. "You've already done something that has helped us more than you will ever know. I'm proud of you, Taka-chan."

"Someday," Father said slowly, "I hope I can return the sword to you, Takao. I would like it to be yours again, one day."

Takao wasn't sure how that would happen, but right now, he wanted to tell the rest of his story.

"Yamaka-san told me to bring you to see him, Father. He said he'd be able to help you. When shall we go?" he asked eagerly. "Shall we go tonight?"

Father began to rub his chin, and Takao knew he was not going to say yes—at least not right away.

"Well," he began, "perhaps Yamaka-san said this just to be polite. After all, why should he want to see me, and how could he possibly help?"

"But I promised," Takao insisted. "You always tell me I should keep my word. He'll be waiting for us."

Father hesitated. "I know . . . I know," he said, and then, as though he had no more words, he added, "Well, we shall see."

That was his way of saying he didn't want to talk about it any more, and Takao knew he would just have to do as Father said. He would have to wait and see.

Father rose to go outside, and he gave Takao a pat on the shoulders. "You're a good lad," he said, and as he went back to the workshop, Takao could hear him call in a happy voice, "I think the tea sets can be saved, after all. My son has just given me a fine surprise!"

And now Mother called him to the kitchen. "You have worked hard, Taka-chan," she said. "Here is a bowl of noodles for you, too."

Mother had filled ten large bowls full of steaming noodles, but as Takao took the first bowl on the tray, she quickly stopped him.

"Not that one, Taka-chan," she said, and she gave him another bowl she had just filled.

Takao grinned as he took it to the table and sat down to eat. It was the only one with an egg floating on top!

That night after supper, Mori-san came over just as soon as he had closed his shop. "I wondered all day about Takao," he said, wiping his face with the corner of his sleeve. He smiled as he saw Takao. "Ah, you are home safe. You were not frightened by the old man?"

Takao shook his head. "He wasn't so bad," he said boldly. "Besides, he bought my sword for 8000 *yen!*"

"Taka-chan wasn't afraid at all," Sumi offered eagerly.

Mori-san nodded. "I knew he had courage," he said. "I knew it when he marched into my shop this morning to sell his beautiful sword!"

Takao didn't know what to do with all this praise. No one had ever told him before that he had courage. He scratched his head and pulled at his ear, and then decided to tell what the old man had said. "Yamaka-san told me to bring Father to see him. He said he could help him," he explained, "but Father won't go with me."

Mr. Mori seemed interested. "Ah, is that so?" he asked. "So the old gentleman said he might help your father?"

Father shook his head. "I am afraid he was just humoring Takao," he said. "I really do not see what he could do in his dark shuttered house to help me."

"Ah, but there may be a way which you do not know," Mori-san said, and he smiled the wise smile of one who knows something and cannot tell. "I am not free to speak of it now," he said, "but I urge you to go see him, Sakata-san. And when you do, why not take some of your pottery to show him?"

"My pottery?" Father asked, puzzled.

Mr. Mori nodded. "It can do no harm, and it may do a great deal of good."

Mori-san seemed to be talking in riddles that

no one understood, but Takao didn't mind as long as he was coaxing Father to go see the old man.

"Will you go then?" Takao asked eagerly. "Will you, Father?"

"If Mori-san thinks it will be helpful," Mother added, "perhaps you should."

"I'll go with you," Sumi said helpfully, "shall I?"

Father thought for a moment, and then answered slowly. "Very well, Takao. I shall go with you, but only after I have seen what I can do about saving the tea sets."

Takao didn't mind waiting for that. "Promise?" he asked.

"It is a promise," Father said.

Mr. Mori looked pleased. "Perhaps this is the beginning of something even better than the selling of the sword," he said. "Takao, I think maybe you have begun something quite wonderful."

"What does Mori-san mean?" Sumi asked curiously.

Takao shrugged. He wondered too, but Mr. Mori would not say, and no one else knew. As Father always said, he would just have to wait and see.

SEVEN

Mr. Kato Confesses

At school, Takao discovered that he had suddenly become quite a hero. No one else in all of Kinrin School had ever had a fire at his house. And, of course, no one had ever had a fire engine roar up to his front door, with firemen carrying hose and hatchets to put out the blaze. Somehow, everyone had heard how Takao ran to the beancurd shop to call for help, and now they said it was Takao who had saved his house.

"I would've stayed that day if you were going to have a fire," Goro said dismally. "It would've been more fun than going to Osaka with Father."

"I didn't know we were going to have a fire," Takao protested. "Besides, that isn't the best part." And he told Goro how he had gone to see the strange old man in the shuttered house.

Goro grinned as he listened. "Aw, now you're just telling a big story," he scoffed. "No one ever goes into that house."

"But I did!" Takao insisted. "And I sold my sword to help Father!"

Now all the boys in class clustered around to listen, and Takao told how he had gone to the shuttered house all alone. He told how the old man had turned out the lights, and how he had finally bought his sword for 8000 *yen*.

Goro whistled and his eyes grew wide. His glasses slipped down his nose, but he was too busy listening to push them up. He scratched his head, and for once he didn't seem to have any words at all. "*Yah*, I sure wouldn't go into that creepy old house by myself," he said, and he looked at Takao with real admiration.

"Me neither," the other boys agreed. "Not for a million *yen*."

Takao shrugged. "Aw, it was easy," he said, and he tried to forget how he had almost crept out of the old man's room in the darkness.

At noon that day, Takao found himself elected captain of the day's baseball team. It didn't seem to make any difference that he hadn't made a single run all semester, and no one even seemed to mind when he struck out in the game with the Sixth Grade boys. At least for now, Takao was a special character around school, and he could do no wrong at all.

In a few days, a new load of kindling arrived, and Father called it "Takao's kindling" because it had been bought with his money. Then Father began once more the firing of the kiln.

"This time, I hope the gods will be kind," Father murmured, and he and Mother took special care to watch the fire carefully.

Takao was careful too. No one had to tell him to stay away. He didn't dare go near the kiln, and he scarcely even looked at Sumi. If anything went wrong this time, he didn't want it to be his fault.

At last, the firing was completed and the kiln was cooled, and when Sumi and Takao came home from school one afternoon, they saw rows and rows of teacups and teapots lined neatly in Father's workshop. They were the soft pale green of winter wheat —exactly the color Father hoped to get.

"Did you save the tea sets, after all?" Takao asked. "Did they come out all right?"

Father nodded. "Thanks to you," he said, "I saved what might have been a big loss."

But Takao saw the frown of worry on Father's

forehead and Sumi asked, "If everything's all right, why do you look so sad?"

"Ah, it is difficult to hide my concern," Father said slowly. "It is just that I wonder now who will buy the tea sets from me."

He did not add that he wondered how he could pay the carpenter for the lumber he had used to rebuild his shed, or how he would pay for the repairs still needed in the workshop before he could work again.

But Mother knew what was heavy in Father's heart, and that night she said, "I wonder if perhaps it is not time now for you to go see Takao's friend. You could surely use some of his help if he is still willing to give it to you."

"Yamaka-san?" Takao asked eagerly. "Do you mean the old man?"

For days Takao had been begging Father to go with him to see the old man, and each time Father had simply said, "Later, Takao. Later . . ." Now, here was Mother herself, suggesting that they go. Takao knew his chance had come, and he grasped it quickly before it should escape.

"Let's go today, Father," he said. "Let's go right now! I'll get my sweater."

But Father would not move that quickly. "Just a minute," he said, holding up a hand. "If we go at all, it won't be till tonight. Yes, perhaps, it would be wise to go tonight," he said.

And after supper, he kept his word.

"I want to go too," Sumi begged. "I'm always getting left out of things. Take me, too!"

But when Takao told her the old man might speak to them in a darkened room with no lights, she quickly changed her mind.

"Maybe I'll wait at home then," she said. "Maybe I'll stay home with Mother."

"I think you are being wise, little one," Father said, and he put on his wool scarf and coat.

"Keep warm now," Mother urged. "Winter is almost here."

Takao nodded as he climbed on the back of Father's bicycle, and Father carefully placed two of his best vases wrapped in a silk *furoshiki* in the basket in front.

"I suppose Mori-san thinks the old man might buy some of my pottery," Father mused almost to himself. "I suppose he is a wealthy old man. Well, we shall see."

And Takao could tell by the tone of his voice that

Father still didn't think the old man would be of any help at all.

The streets were dark and empty as they headed toward the temple, and a cold wind swept down from the gray mountains that circled the city. Father tightened his scarf as he pumped against the wind, and Takao clung tight to him so he wouldn't fall off. All the shops were boarded up for the night, and they passed only the noodle vendor who rode by on his bicycle, blowing a sad lonely tune on his whistle.

"A bowl of noodles sure would taste good now, wouldn't it?" Takao murmured.

Father kept right on pumping, not even turning to look.

"It'd be nice and warm," Takao added a bit louder. But still Father did not answer. It seemed he had something on his mind, but it was clearly not a bowl of noodles.

As they neared the temple, Takao could see its five-storied tower looming dark and tall over the wooded hillside. The wind sighed through the pine trees and made them shiver softly. Even the light of the sky seemed to be shut off, as clouds gathered darkly across the pale autumn moon. The bicycle

crunched up the graveled path and over the dry dead leaves that had fluttered from the maple trees. Takao shivered. He was glad he was not alone this time.

When Father pressed the small bell at Yamaka-san's gate, Takao heard again the scraping of the *geta* and the thin high voice asking, *"Hai?* Who is it?" Her voice sounded lonely in the darkness of the silent night.

"It is Sakata, the potter," Father said. "My son sold a sword to your master, and I believe he wished to see me."

The young girl opened the door quickly. "*Dozo,* come in," she said with a bow. "The master said I should expect you one day."

She led the way to the house, and this time she took them to the front entrance and asked them to wait.

In a moment she was back. "Please, follow me," she said, and she led them to the same room where Takao had been before. The old man looked as though he had not moved at all.

Father bowed carefully to the floor. "I am afraid my son was a great nuisance to you," he apologized.

The old man scarcely bothered to return his bow. "So, you are the father who was helped by this boy," he said. "And your pots?" he asked. "Did you save your pots?"

"I did," Father answered, "thanks to your help."

The old man waved away his thanks with an impatient hand. "Ah, you have brought some of your pottery," he said, glancing at the *furoshiki* bundle.

Takao was amazed at the old man. He seemed to be able to see right through the cloth.

"They are not very new pieces," Father explained. "I have been occupied with a rush order for some tea sets and could do nothing else."

Suddenly, the old man sat up and seemed enormously interested. "Tea sets, did you say?" he asked.

"For old Kato-san from Gojo Hill," Takao interrupted. "But now he's mad and he'll never come back."

"Tell me about this Kato and about your rush order," the old man said quickly. He leaned forward now to hear each word.

Father seemed puzzled, but he did as he was told. He told how Kato-san had come and demanded the twenty-five sets in less than three weeks.

The old man's face clouded with anger as he listened. "The scoundrel," he murmured. "The scheming, lying scoundrel!"

"You are acquainted with Kato-san?" Father ventured.

And it was then that Takao and Father learned at last what Mr. Mori had known and not been able to tell.

"Not only am I acquainted with Kato," the old man said, "I have employed him for the past seven years to handle the business of my Gojo Hill shops."

"Your shops!" Takao and Father said almost at the same time.

"Then, it was for you that I made those tea sets?" Father asked.

The old man shook his head. "When I asked Kato to find me a potter who could make them, he said he could find no one who could do the work in such a short time. He caused me to lose a very big order." The old man thought for a moment, tugging at his beard, and then added, "But you say you made them!"

Mr. Yamaka suddenly rose in a rustle of soft silk. He clapped for his maid and ordered her to fetch Mr. Kato. "Tell him to come immediately," he commanded. "He has some explaining to do."

Takao's head began to whirl. The old man owned the shops on Gojo Hill and Kato-san had been working for him all along. It was like a strange mixed-up dream, and Takao wondered if Mr. Kato might not come creeping in on five pair of legs, breathing fire and dragging a thorny tail.

Mr. Kato came at last, walking only on two legs and breathless from having hurried. He took one look at Father and Takao, and his mouth fell open as though he had just seen his ancestors back from their graves.

The old man glared at him. "Well, what have you to say for yourself?" he asked. "Sakata-san has told me all about the tea sets."

Mr. Kato wiped his face with a big white handkerchief. Then, stammering and stuttering, he confessed everything. He had lied to the old man. He had forced Father to rush with the tea sets so he could sell them to the American customer and take the money for himself. But the fire had spoiled his plans and his little scheme had failed after all.

"Please forgive me," he murmured, bowing to Yamaka-san. "I promise I shall never deceive you again."

"That is indeed correct," the old man said, "because you will never have the chance. You are dismissed as of this moment, and I never want to see your miserable face again. Now get out!"

Takao felt as though he were watching a paper show come to life. The villain bowed and scraped and edged miserably out of the room. And the old man—the hero—brushed his hands, as though he had just finished a disagreeable job. He shook his head and said, "I have been a great fool."

Then, he clapped for the maid and ordered some tea.

"You must not bother with us," Father said quickly. "We must leave soon, for Takao must get up tomorrow morning for school."

"But I'm not sleepy at all, Father," Takao said quickly. "I'll be able to get up tomorrow!" How could he possibly think of leaving now, just when things were getting interesting and the old man had even sent for tea.

"The tea is as much for myself as it is for you," the old man said matter-of-factly. "This is a celebration. I have just decided to end my retirement. I was a fool to think I could trust Kato to manage my shops. It is time I came out once more into the world."

"And opened your shutters?" Takao asked.

Father put a hand on his shoulder to silence him, but the old man nodded. "I have been in the darkness for seven years, mourning the death of my beloved wife," he said. "Until now, only Kato and my friend Mori-san knew. But now, I shall begin a new life. I shall open the shutters to the world and I shall run my own business once more."

Takao had never heard the old man speak so many words before. He seemed almost like a different person.

"It will be a fine thing," Father said. "A fine thing indeed."

The maid came in now with the tea and placed before each of them a small porcelain cup on a saucer of wood. Takao was thirsty. He took a big gulp and then didn't know what to do. The tea was so bitter and so strong, he could scarcely swallow it. His mouth puckered into an "o," and he felt as though he had just eaten a big green persimmon. Takao quickly took one of the small sugared apricots from the silver bowl to take away the taste of the tea, but it was so terribly sour, instead of helping, it made him shiver and suck in his breath and blink back a rush of quick tears.

He looked up to see the old man pop three into his mouth all at once. "My favorite sweet," he said calmly, and he ate them without blinking an eye.

Takao glanced at Father and saw that he actually enjoyed this dreadful tea. "Ah, a fine cup of tea," he murmured, and he sipped it slowly to enjoy its flavor.

Takao sighed. Tea at the old man's house was as strange as everything else about him. Takao was ready to go home now, and he gave Father's sleeve a quick tug.

The old man's eyes were sharp. "Ah, you are ready to go now, are you?" he asked. "But first, I must speak to your father of business."

He looked carefully at the vases Father had brought and murmured, "Your work is very fine indeed. Bring your tea sets to my shop tomorrow. I think I might be able to buy them all."

Father bowed. "You are very kind," he said. "It is good to have hope for the future again."

Now Takao knew what Mr. Mori had meant that night. If the old man would buy Father's pottery, then surely this was the wonderful thing, better even than the selling of the sword!

When Takao and Father left for home, the night

seemed even darker and colder than before. But somehow, the way did not seem lonely at all, for Father was happy and he whistled all the way home.

"You and Grandfather's sword have indeed begun something very wonderful," Father said as they reached the front gate. "And don't think I've forgotten what I said about the sword," he added. "It may take a few years, but I'm going to buy it back for you someday, and that's a promise."

Father never made a promise he could not keep. Takao felt sure now that the sword would come back to him someday, and when it did, everything would be wonderful, not just for Father, but for him, too.

EIGHT

The Old Man Pays a Debt

Takao sat at the table beside Goro and looked at the clock. It was almost five o'clock and time to be going home.

"Come on, Goro," he coaxed once more. "Trade me one of your Swedish stamps for my American one."

Goro shook his head. "The Swedish ones are harder to get," he said firmly.

"But mine isn't even canceled," Takao went on. "It's brand new."

Goro looked at it for a moment and then shook his head. "Uh-un," he said. "Offer me something else."

Takao just didn't have enough extra stamps to offer a better trade. It was no use trying to make Goro change his mind. "Well, I guess I'll go home then," he said pensively. "It's almost time for supper anyway."

But Goro wanted Takao to stay. He asked once more about the old man, for Takao had told him how he and Father had gone to see him. "Is your Father really going to make pottery for him now?" Goro asked.

Takao nodded. "Looks like," he answered. "He bought all the tea sets Father brought him."

"All twenty-five?"

"Sure," Takao went on. "That's why we had red bean rice and sea bream for supper last night. Father said it was a real celebration."

Goro swallowed at the thought of broiled sea bream. "And are you going up to see the old man again sometime?" he asked.

Takao remembered what Father had said about his sword. "Maybe," he answered cautiously. "Maybe we'll go again to buy back my sword."

"Aw, how could you do that?" Goro asked. "If the old man collects swords, he won't give yours back, will he?"

Takao frowned. "But Father promised," he insisted. "I'll get it back someday. You'll see."

Goro was silent for a while and then he asked slowly, "You still want to trade for that Swedish stamp?"

"Sure I do," Takao said eagerly.

"All right then," Goro said. "I'll trade if you'll let me go with you the next time you go see the old man."

"Sure," Takao agreed. "That's easy." He gave his stamp to Goro and carefully took the Swedish stamp in return. It was a beauty, and Takao could hardly wait to get it in his album.

"Thanks a lot," he called as he left for home.

"Don't forget what you promised," Goro reminded him.

"I won't," Takao called back.

He hurried now, for the winter sky was dark, and already a single star had appeared over the tip of Mt. Hiei. Sumi had probably set the table by now, and Mother probably had bean soup bubbling on the charcoal cooker.

Takao ran lightly, thinking again of his promise to Goro, and a slow smile spread over his face. At last, it was his turn to be doing things Goro could never do. Now, Goro was the one to be envious. Maybe I could even beat him in a race now, Takao thought grandly, and with a sudden spurt, he ran all the way home.

The third week of December, schools closed for winter recess, and one day, when Takao came home from Goro's, he saw that Mother had begun her year-end cleaning. She was using a brand-new broom she had bought from the peddler and was sweeping away the dust and dirt of the old year.

"We'll have to scrub the *tatami* and polish the woodwork too," she said to Takao as he came in. "And I want you and Sumi-chan to clean out your drawers and line them with fresh paper."

Takao pretended he hadn't heard and tiptoed to his desk. He got out his magnifying glass and examined the cicada in his insect collection. He'd have to catch a better specimen next summer, he thought.

"Takao," Mother said.

"*Hai?*"

"Did you hear what I said?"

"Yes," Takao admitted dismally.

"Then suppose you begin with your drawers now," Mother went on.

Takao groaned. This was the part of the holidays he didn't like at all.

"But we just cleaned the whole house when we had the fire," he complained. The smoke had covered everything then with thick black dust.

Mother paid no attention to him. She simply brought a bucket of hot water and told Takao to scrub the *tatami* in his room when he had finished his drawers. There was no getting out of it. This was just one of the bad things that came with New Year's just as surely as the wonderful squares of toasted rice cakes.

Two days before New Year's, Mother began to prepare the delicious food she would put in her three-tiered boxes for the New Year feast. This was the nice part—the part Takao liked best. And when all sorts of wonderful smells began to drift through the house, Takao wouldn't go out even to see Goro. Somehow, both he and Sumi found any number of things to do at home, and furthermore, they found it necessary to pass the kitchen dozens of times. Then, they would look in and beg for just one small slice of lotus root or just one mouthful of the sweet chestnut paste Mother was making.

At last, on the afternoon of the thirty-first day, Mother announced there could be no more sampling. "Tomorrow you shall have as much as you wish," she said firmly, "but no more today."

Then, she told Sumi to go outside and Takao to

go for his haircut and bath. Mother usually cut Takao's hair, but at New Year's he was always sent to the barber.

Takao rubbed the bristles on top of his head. "I don't need a haircut yet," he muttered.

But Mother was determined. "You must begin the new year with a clean mind and body," she said. "And besides, I want you to look your best when you make your calls tomorrow."

"Where will he go?" Sumi wanted to know. "What calls does he have to make?"

"Why, he and Father must go to thank Mori-san," Mother explained. "After all, if he had not sent Takao to Yamaka-san's, Father might not be selling his pottery today."

"And the old man?" Takao asked. "Will we go see him too?"

"Of course," Mother answered. "You and Father must go pay your respects to him too. Perhaps you could take him a basket of fruit."

Takao didn't have to hear any more. "I'll go for a haircut then," he said quickly. And when he was finished, he ran as fast as he could to see Goro.

"Come to the bath with me," he urged.

But Goro wasn't very interested. "I'm fixing my

kite for tomorrow," he said. "It needs a new tail."

"Aw, you'll get a new one tomorrow," Takao answered. Everybody got a new kite at New Year's. "Besides," he went on, "if you don't go take a bath now, you'll just have to go later."

Goro nodded. "I know," he said. His mother would surely send him later if he did not go now.

"Besides, I've got something important to tell you," Takao added. He wanted to save the good news for later—like a piece of candy that can be enjoyed in one's pocket for a long while before it is actually eaten.

"Well, all right then," Goro said at last. "I'll go." And he hurried to get his towel and his soap.

The Public Bath was just as crowded as the barber shop had been. Everybody wanted to get clean for the first day of the new year.

Goro nudged Takao as they waited to get in. "Tell me now," he urged. "What is it that's so important?"

And so Takao told how he and Father would be going to pay their respects to Mr. Yamaka the very next morning. "I haven't forgotten what I promised," Takao said. "Want to come with us?"

"Do I?" Goro answered. He was so excited, he

nearly swung his soap right out of his tin bath pail. "I sure am glad I have you for a friend," he said enthusiastically. And when they got inside, he gave Takao the best back-scrubbing he'd had in a long while.

Goro and Takao decided to walk home through the market place so they could see all the vendors who had come from the country to sell pine branches and juicy tangerines and special decorations for the front gate. They pushed their way through the crowds, jostling mothers with bulging market baskets on their arms and babies bundled up in small quilts and strapped to their backs.

They stopped to watch the woman who made rice flour cakes, sniffing the sweet dough as it sizzled and rose into round puffy cakes. Takao dug his hands deep into his pockets, but they were as empty as two old socks. He glanced at Goro, but Goro shook his head. "I don't have a single *yen*," he said glumly.

"Well, let's go home then," Takao suggested. "Maybe if you come, Mother will give us something good to eat."

They had almost reached Takao's house when they heard the car behind them. It wasn't often that cars came down their street, and the driver honked his horn to get them out of his way. Takao and Goro took their time and edged slowly to the side of the road. The big black car passed by, and a head popped out of the window to shout at them.

"Foolish children," a voice called. "You'll be hit someday if you can't move faster than that!"

There was something familiar about that voice, and when Takao looked closely, he knew why. "That's Yamaka-san!" he shouted. "It's the old man," he said, nudging Goro.

They began to run after the car, but they didn't have to run far, for the car slowed down and then came to a full stop right in front of Takao's house.

"Yamaka-san!" Takao shouted. "What are you doing here?"

A chauffeur opened the door and helped the old man out. He wore a big black cape over his *kimono* and a brown beaver hat with flaps that came down over his ears to keep out the noise. He leaned on a thin cane and carried a long *furoshiki* bundle in his other hand. The old man squinted at Takao.

"Ah, so it is my young friend," he said. "I have seen you only in the darkness and did not know you in the light of day."

"Maybe because I just got a haircut," Takao said helpfully. "And besides, I just took a bath. This is my friend, Goro. He just took a bath, too," he explained.

The old man smiled. "Ah, you are both ready to welcome the new year properly. That is good. Now, I should like to enter your house."

Takao ran in ahead to call Mother and Father. "He's here! He's come here!" he shouted. "He came in a big black car!"

Sumi put down her crayons and looked up. "Who?" she asked. "Who came in a black car?"

Mother hurried from the kitchen, wiping her hands on her apron. "Who is it, Takao? What are you shouting about?"

By the time Takao called Father from the workshop, the old man had grown impatient and had already removed his *geta* and stepped into the house.

It was only after he was seated on the best cushion, nearest the *hibachi,* and nearest the special alcove, however, that Mother and Father bowed to welcome him.

"It is indeed an honor," they said. "We are so grateful to have you come to our humble home."

The old man did not like all the bowing. "No,

no," he said. "I am the grateful one. I have come to pay a debt before the new year."

Father looked puzzled. "A debt?" he asked. "But I have already been paid for my pottery. You owe me nothing."

The old man shook his head. "The debt is not owed to you, but to your son."

It was Takao's turn now to be puzzled. "To me?" he asked. "What for?"

"For freeing me from my tomb," Mr. Yamaka said. "If you had not come to me with your sword, I would still be sitting in the darkness, still deceived by Kato, and doing nothing but waiting for death. I am grateful you had the courage to come to my shuttered house. I am glad you wanted to help your father."

He slid the long *furoshiki* bundle toward Takao now and said, "Because I want to thank you, I have brought a gift. It is one I think you deserve, and I hope it brings you the good fortune it brought me."

Takao bowed to thank him. He reached out to touch the knot of the *furoshiki* when he heard Mother cough lightly. He knew it was not proper to open a gift the moment it was given to you, but how could he possibly wait till the old man had gone home?

"Taka-chan, will you get more charcoal for the *hibachi?*" Mother asked quietly. She was telling Takao that he must be polite and wait.

By the time Takao returned with the charcoal, Mother was serving tea and sweet cakes and sugared *azuki* beans, and the old man talked with Father of the new vases he would make for his shop.

Goro edged closer to Takao as they drank their tea. "What do you suppose is in there?" he whispered, glancing at the *furoshiki* bundle.

"I've an idea," Takao answered, "but I'm not sure."

The old man finally finished his tea and ate the last red bean on his dish when Sumi sighed and spoke in a voice everyone could hear.

"I wonder what's in the package for Takao," she said, tipping her head as she gazed at the long bundle.

"*Mah,* Sumi-chan!" Mother said with an embarrassed look.

But Takao grinned. For once Sumi had said just the right thing at the right time. Takao thought he would explode if he had to wait another minute to open his package. He looked at the old man and saw him nod.

"Never mind being polite," Yamaka-san said. "Open it."

Takao didn't have to be coaxed. In a minute, he untied the *furoshiki* and knew he had guessed right. It was a sword box, just as he'd thought. And when he lifted the lid, there was Grandfather's sword, just as he had taken it to the old man, wrapped carefully in a cloth of red silk.

"Father, look!" Takao said happily. "It came back after all, just like you said!"

"*Mah,*" Mother gasped. "We could not have asked for anything more."

Father bowed as he thanked the old man. "You understood my heart well," he said. "It was my hope that I could one day return the sword to Takao. I hope he will be worthy of your gift."

The old man looked at Father. "Of course, he will," he said, "because I expect it of him."

Takao was too excited to notice the thoughtful expression on Father's face.

"Look, Goro," he said. "Didn't I tell you I'd get it back?"

Goro took the sword in his hands and turned it over and over. "*Yah,* I'd sure like to have a sword like this," he said with a sigh. "You sure have all the luck!"

"I'll say," Sumi agreed wistfully.

But Mother added, "I think Takao deserved it this time. I'm glad the sword came back to him in time for the new year."

The old man nodded. "It is back where it belongs, and I, too, must go to my home. My debt is paid. Now, I shall go call on Mori-san and then I can welcome the new year with a peaceful heart."

As the old man rose to go, Takao told him he would see him again the next day. "I'm coming for a New Year's call," he said eagerly, "with Father and Goro."

"Very well," the old man said, "I shall expect you then," and with a soft chuckle he added, "Perhaps I can find more sugared apricots for you!"

He climbed into his big black car and then he was gone, and Takao heard only the honking of the horn as the car disappeared into the shadows of the street.

That night, Mother made her usual passing-of-the-year noodles, and at nine o'clock, she carried out four steaming bowls.

"But Mother," Sumi objected, "we shouldn't be

eating this till midnight when the old year passes."

"And by that time, little one," Father said, "you will be sound asleep."

Sumi wrinkled her nose. "Then, can't I wait up to hear the midnight bells?" she asked, disappointed.

"Not yet, Sumi-chan," Mother said. "You must wait until you are a little older."

Takao decided it was time to try his luck. "But I'm old enough now, aren't I?" he asked.

He waited for Father to shake his head as usual and say it was more important for him to get to sleep so he could wake up bright and early the next morning. But this was a day full of surprises, and Father gave him still another one.

"I think you might stay up if you like," he said. "I think you are old enough now."

What an amazing day this was! Even the noodles tasted better than they ever had before.

Sumi went to bed gloomily and was cheered only when Mother told her she would find a new silk *kimono* at the foot of her quilts when she woke up the next morning.

Takao moved close to the *hibachi* and warmed his hands on its smooth rounded rim. Mother mended one last sock before the old year was gone, and Father finished reading the evening paper. The house was filled again with a feeling of waiting, but this time, it was a peaceful, happy waiting that held no fear.

"It was a good year after all, wasn't it?" Mother said thoughtfully, as she made the final knot in her thread. "The fire was a dreadful thing, but it actually brought so much that was good."

"Like getting rid of old Kato-san," Takao said.

"And bringing Yamaka-san to us instead," Mother agreed.

Father folded his paper and put it on the table. "I have been doing some thinking about my work," he said slowly. "With so many new orders from Yamaka-san's shop, I believe I could use more help in the workshop."

Takao sat up and listened closely as Father went on.

"Mother has enough to do in the house cooking and washing and cleaning for us," he began, and then, turning to Takao, he added, "How would you like to help me a little each afternoon beginning with the new year?"

Takao had to make sure he had heard what

Father said. "You mean I can really help you?" he asked. "Is it time now?"

Father nodded. "I think it is time now," he said. "It is as the old man said, if I expect it of you, you will be able to do the work. I will have faith in you."

Takao leaped up in his excitement and nearly knocked the kettle from the top of the *hibachi*. "*Yah,* wait till I tell Goro!" he said happily. "Will he be surprised!" Now, at last, he could make up for the lie to Goro, for this time he would really be helping Father.

Father and Mother talked of Father's work, and of how they might finish repairing the workshop after the holidays. And as Takao listened, their voices grew farther and farther away. He wasn't sure what happened after that, for the next thing he knew, Father was shaking him by the shoulders.

"Listen," he whispered softly. "It's midnight."

Takao sat very still and listened. Faintly at first, and then growing louder, he heard all the bells of Kyoto's temples ringing out over the city. They were ringing out the evil and the sadness of the old year and ringing in the good of the new.

In front of him, on the alcove, Takao saw Grandfather's sword. It was just as the old man had said. It had brought him good fortune already, and somehow Takao had the feeling Grandfather knew all about it. Perhaps he had known all along that someday the sword would bring Takao the promise of the best new year he'd ever had.

GLOSSARY

Atsui	ah-tsoo-ee
Azuki	ah-zoo-kee
Chan	chahn
Dozo	doh-zoh
Furoshiki	foo-roh-shee-kee
Geta	geh-tah
Hai	hai
Hibachi	hee-bah-chee
Kimono	kee-moh-noh
Kon nichi wa	kon-nee-chee-wah
Kora	koh-rah
Mah	mah
Namu Amida Butsu	nah-moo ah-mee-dah boo-tsoo
Sah	sah
Samurai	sah-moo-rai
San	sahn
Suzuri	soo-zoo-ree
Tabi	tah-bee
Tadaima	tah-dah-ee-mah
Tatami	tah-tah-mee
Yah	yah
Yai	yai
Yen	yen
Yoisho	yoi-sho

hot

small red beans

Usually added to a child's name when speaking to him. It is a little like calling a boy named Bill, Billy.

please

a square cloth used to wrap and carry small articles

wooden clogs

yes

a brazier

a Japanese dress

"How do you do"

an exclamation, like "Hey!"

"My!"

"May Buddha be praised."

"Well!"

a Japanese warrior of olden days

Used after a name, it can mean Mr., Mrs., or Miss.

A rectangular stone with a polished surface, on which an ink stick is rubbed to make black *sumi* ink. There is a shallow trough on one end for water.

Japanese socks

"I'm home!"

a woven rush mat laid over the floor of most Japanese houses

an exclamation

an exclamation

a unit of Japanese money similar to our dollar

an exclamation